Not Me!

by Nigel McMullen

Albury Children's

Jack says Kenny is the best brother in the world.

At breakfast, when Jack knocked his plate on the floor and Mom came in looking cross...

This book belongs to....

_____

_____

For Jack Kitchin
and his Mum and Dad

N.McM.

First published in 2001

This edition published in 2017 by Albury Books
Albury Court, Thame, Oxfordshire, OX9 2LP
United Kingdom

Text and illustrations © Nigel McMullen 2001

A CIP record for this title is available from the British Library.

The right of Nigel McMullen to be identified
as the author and illustrator of this work has been asserted by him
in accordance with the Copyright, Designs, and Patents Act, 1988.

ISBN 978-1-910235-32-4

Printed and bound in Turkey

For orders: Kuperard Publishers and Distributors +44 (0) 208 4462440

Jack said,
"It was him!"

Kenny, who was too young to talk,
said nothing.

At lunchtime, when Mom asked who had eaten the cake she'd taken all morning to make...

Jack said, "Not me!"
and hid the last slice in Kenny's diaper.

Kenny, who was too young to care, sat down.

Jack was building mudpies
when Mom called,
"You'd better stay clean!"

Jack said, "I will,"
and cleaned his hands on Kenny's shirt.

Kenny, who was too young to
know what mud was,
**thought it
tasted lovely.**

At bathtime,
Jack was playing with
the squirty soap when
Mom asked who'd
made all the mess...

Jack said,
"It was him!"
and handed the bottle
to Kenny.

Kenny, who was too young to know better, squirted Mom.

When they were warm and sleepy and ready for bed, Mom looked at Kenny and sighed, "You're so much trouble! But we wouldn't swap him, would we, Jack?"

Jack said, "Not me," and gave Kenny a kiss.

Kenny, who had never said anything before,
chose that moment to say

his very first word…

Other books for you to enjoy...

My Mom
Beth Shoshan & Jacqueline East
My Mom is amazing; You'll be so impressed. Now follow this story, You'll see she's the best! A sweet and gentle story, celebrating the love between a mother and her child.

Mess Monsters
Beth Shoshan & Piers Harper
There are Mess Monsters under the bed. When they're out, they'll smash, they'll crash, they'll bang and clang, stamp and stomp. Most of all they'll make a mess. But the Mess Monsters haven't met Mommy yet...

My Perfect Pet
Stuart Trotter
Can you guess which is the perfect pet - one that's not dry and not at all wet, not too hairy and not too scary, not too slinky and not too stinky? With its simple rhymes and bold, exciting pictures, 'My Perfect Pet' will delight young children time and time again.

Lulubell Ladybug
Sam Walshaw
Mrs. Ladybug is very busy. With so many children there's always so much to do! Thank goodness for caring Lulubell who steps in and helps in a way only Lulubell can... Lovely, colourful pictures illustrate this charming story for the very young.